This book belongs to

....

Written by Rosie Greening.
Illustrated by Clare Fennell.

The Christmas SELFIE Contest

Rosie Greening • Clare Fennell

make
believe
ideas

In a big, busy workshop
with shelves full of toys,
the elves worked their socks off
and made lots of noise!

They hammered and clattered and chattered and played,

and worked as a team on the toys that they made.

But Alfie was different
to all of the rest.
He didn't like teamwork:
he liked being best!

He'd boast about all of the toys he'd create,

then show them to everyone, shouting, "I'M GREAT!"

One morning, the elves
were so sick of his talk,
the Head Elf said:

"Alfie, please
go for a walk!"

So Alfie went out
to the gingerbread store,
and noticed a poster
he'd not seen before . . .

Best Selfie

It said:

Santa is holding a

SELFIE CONTEST

so send in your photos and he'll pick the best.

Young Alfie was certain he'd win it with ease.

"I'll take the best selfie –
it sounds like a breeze."

He told all his **friends**,
and they just got **annoyed**:
"There's no time for **selfies** –
we **need** to make **toys**!"

SANTA'S WORKSHOP

But Alfie ignored them and all of their fears.
He needed to try out some selfie ideas.

He ran to the polar bears chilling outside.
"Please pose for a selfie!" he eagerly cried.

The bears made a tower and Alfie yelled, "CHEESE!"
But one of the polar bears just . . . had . . . to . . . SNEEZE!

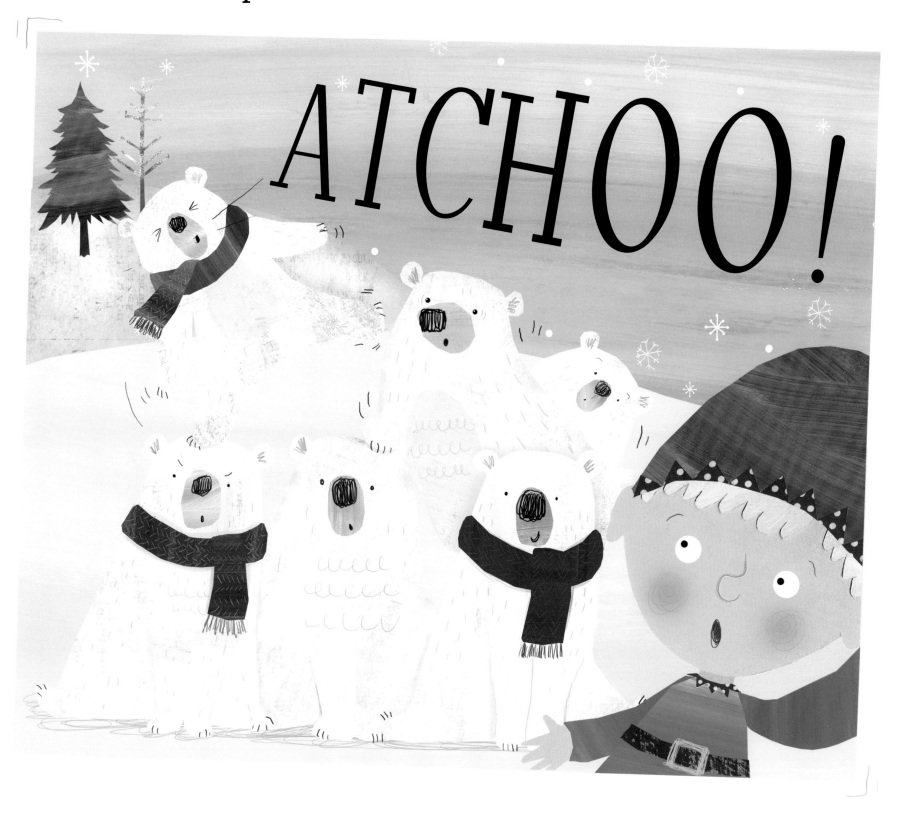

ATCHOO!

So Alfie rushed off to a whale in the sea.

He said, "Will you pose for a selfie with me?"

But as Alfie's camera went off with a flash,

the whale spurted water on him with a SPLASH!

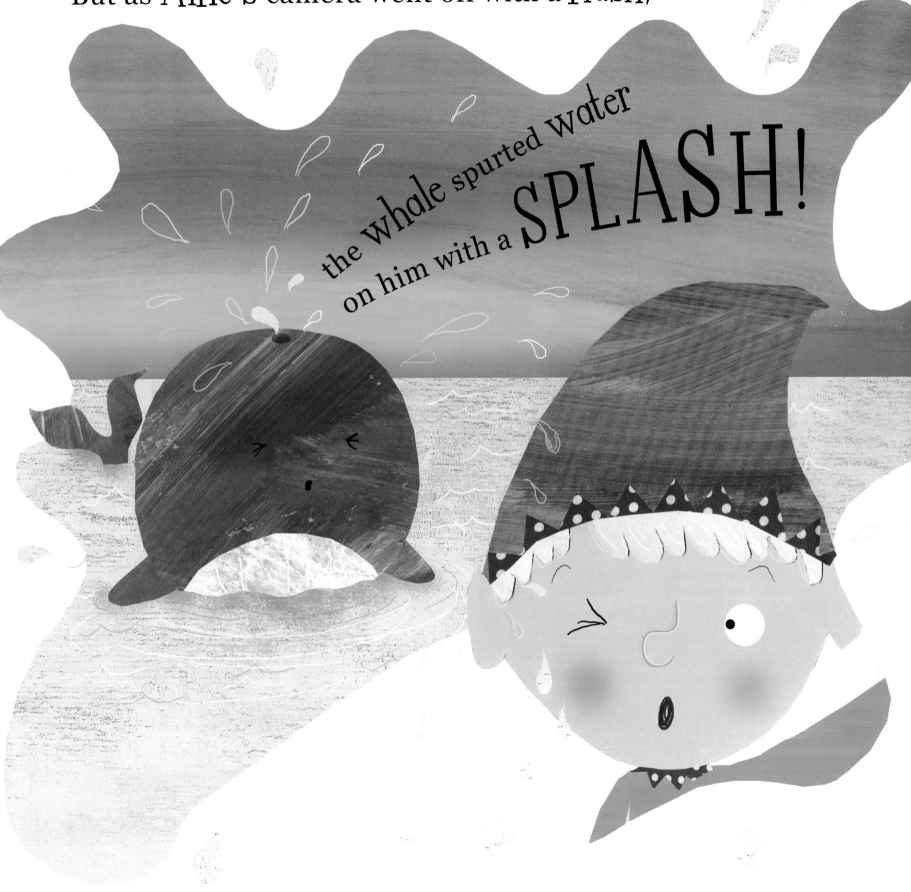

Then as it grew darker,
two owls fluttered past.

"Will you take a selfie with me?"
Alfie asked.

The group had a **hoot,**
but it still wouldn't do . . .

the sky was too dark . . .

and the selfies were too!

Poor Alfie ran back
to the workshop in tears.
"I thought I would win,
but I'm out of ideas!"

"Forget about selfies," the other elves said.

"Let's finish these toys with some teamwork instead!"

The elves got to work
and at last Alfie saw . . .

when they worked
as a **team**,
they could do
so much more.

TOYS

They **sanded** and **painted**

with painstaking care,

and soon there were

colourful toys everywhere!

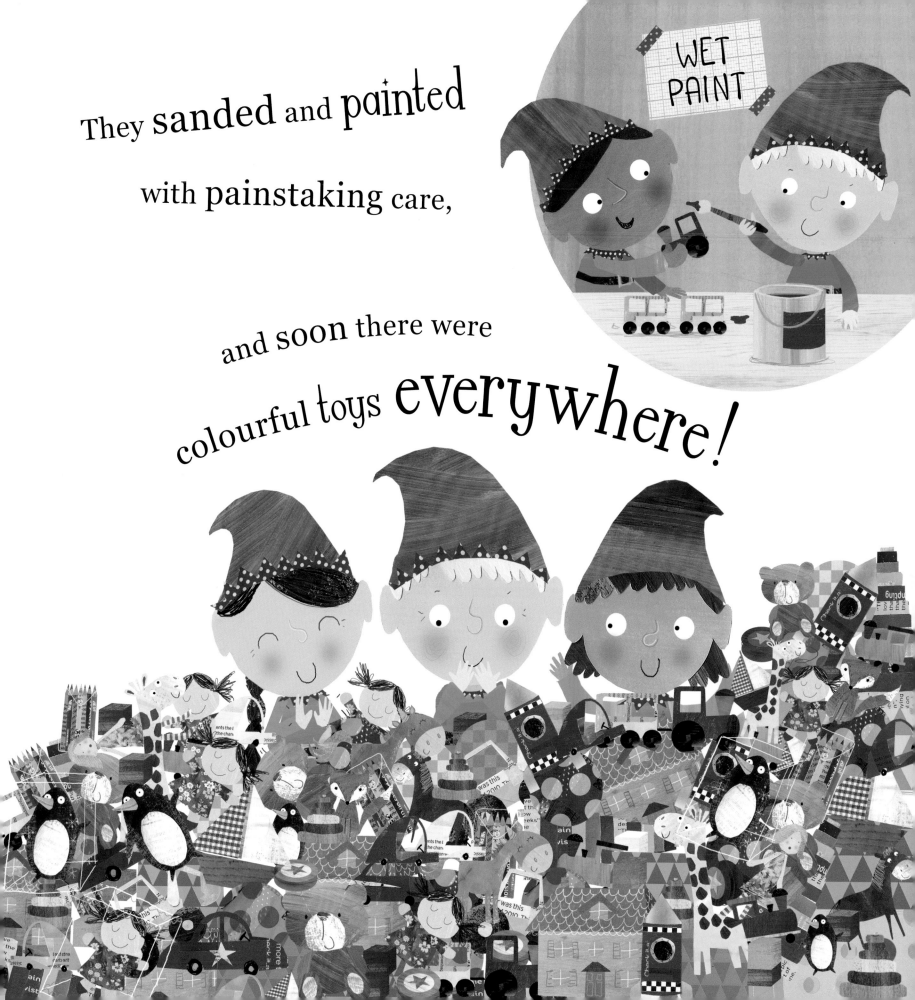

"The workshop looks magical!"
young Alfie said.

And then an idea popped into his head . . .

"Let's pose for a selfie!"

he said with a grin.

"With all of us in it, this selfie could win!"

He sent off the selfie and to his surprise,

he got a reply saying:

You've won first prize!

I LOVE SANTA!

1st

Your prize is a sleigh ride

with Santa himself.

Congrats on your selfie –

you're one lucky elf!

Young **Alfie** was thrilled,
and he **knew** what to do.
He showed all his **friends**
and said, "You should come too!"

When Santa arrived in his beautiful sleigh, the elves clambered in, then they went on their way.

And as Santa's reindeer soared into the skies,
young Alfie was glad they had all shared his prize!

THE END